Swing, Swing, Swing

Written by Gail Tuchman

Pictures by Shelley Dieterichs

SCHOLASTIC INC.

New York   Toronto   London   Auckland   Sydney

Copyright © 1994 by Scholastic Inc.
All rights reserved. Published by Scholastic Inc.
Printed in the U.S.A.
ISBN 0-590-27556-9

3 4 5 6 7 8 9 10   09   00 99 98 97 96 95 94

Swing, swing, swing.

My swing is so big
I'll get my frog.

My frog will swing with me.

My swing is so big
I'll get my cat.

My cat will swing with me.

My swing is so big
I'll get my dog.

My dog will swing with me.

My swing is so big
I'll get my goose.

My goose will swing with me.

My swing is so big
I'll get my horse.

My horse will swing with me.

My swing is so small
there's no room at all.

I think I'll swing alone!